A Christmas Carol

A Christmas Carol

by CHARLES DICKENS

Retold and Illustrated by
JAMES RICE

PELICAN PUBLISHING COMPANY
GRETNA 1990

Copyright © 1990
By Pelican Publishing Company, Inc.

Library of Congress Cataloging-in-Publication Data

Dickens, Charles, 1812-1870.
  A Christmas carol / by Charles Dickens ; retold and illustrated by
James Rice.
    p. cm.
  Summary: A retelling of the Dickens classic.
  ISBN 0-88289-812-4
  [1. Christmas--Fiction. 2. Ghosts--Fiction.] I. Rice, James,
1934- ill. II. Title.
PZ7.D55Cew 1990c
[E]--dc20
                                                        90-39341
                                                           CIP
                                                            AC

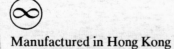

Manufactured in Hong Kong

Published by Pelican Publishing Company, Inc.
1101 Monroe Street, Gretna, Louisiana 70053

Marley was dead. The sign over the door said SCROOGE AND MARLEY. Marley had been dead for seven years but Scrooge had never painted out old Marley's name.

Ebenezer Scrooge was a squeezing, wrenching, tight-fisted old sinner. No one liked him or even spoke to him and Scrooge didn't care.

It was a cold Christmas Eve—Scrooge sat busy in his counting-house. He had a very small fire, but the clerk's fire was so very much smaller that it looked like one coal. But he couldn't replenish it, for Scrooge kept the coal-box in his own room.

"A Merry Christmas, uncle! God save you!" cried Scrooge's nephew as he entered the office. "Bah!" said Scrooge; "humbug!" He refused an invitation to Christmas dinner.

Scrooge likewise dismissed two men asking for donations to the poor. He said the poor would be better dead to reduce the population.

At closing time the clerk asked off the following day. "It's only once a year, sir."

"A poor excuse for picking a man's pocket every twenty-fifth of December! Be here all the earlier *next* morning," Scrooge growled .

Scrooge went home to a dark, dreary old apartment that had belonged to his partner, Jacob Marley.

As he opened the door, Marley's face appeared—then disappeared—on the door knocker.

He closed the door with a bang. The sound resounded through the house like thunder. Every room above, and every cask in the wine-merchant's cellar below, appeared to have a separate peal of echoes. Scrooge was not a man to be frightened by echoes. He fastened the door, and walked across the hall, and up the stairs. Slowly too, trimming his candle as he went.

Up Scrooge went, not caring a button for its being very dark. Darkness is cheap, and Scrooge liked it. But before he shut his heavy door, he walked through his rooms to see that all was right. He had just enough recollection of the face in the knocker to desire to do that.

Sitting-room, bedroom, lumber-room, all as they should be. Nobody under the table, nobody under the sofa; a small fire in the grate; spoon and basin ready. Quite satisfied, he closed his door.

His glance happened to rest upon a disused bell that hung in the room. With a strange dread he saw the bell begin to swing. Soon it rang out loudly, as did every bell in the house.

Deep down below came a clanking noise as if someone were dragging a heavy chain. The noise grew louder coming up the stairs straight toward his door.

It came on through the heavy door, and a specter passed into the room before his eyes. And upon its coming in, the dying flame leaped up, as though it cried, "I know him! Marley's ghost!"

The same face, the very same, but his body was transparent. He had death-cold eyes, and a folded kerchief was bound about his head and chin.

Scrooge asked, "Why do spirits walk the earth, and why do they come to me?" "If a man's spirit does not go forth in life, it is condemned to do so after death," Marley's ghost replied.

"You have yet a chance of escaping my fate. You will be haunted by Three Spirits during the next three nights. Without their visits, you cannot hope to shun the path I tread," said the ghost, and he vanished.

Scrooge went straight to bed to try to sleep. When the clock struck one, a light flashed and the curtains of his bed were drawn aside by a strange figure: the Ghost of Christmas Past. The Ghost's hair, which hung about its neck and down its back, was white as if with age; and yet the face had not a wrinkle in it, and the tenderest bloom was on the skin.

The Ghost said, "I will show you shadows of the things that have been." "Why?" "For your welfare. Rise and walk with me! Those we see can neither see nor hear us." They passed through the wall and back in time.

Scrooge soon saw himself as a youth apprenticed to Fezziwig, the shopkeeper. Fezziwig was happily preparing for Christmas. A fiddler and guests entered and everyone danced and celebrated.

There were more dances. Then old Fezziwig stood out to dance with Mrs. Fezziwig.

There were three and twenty pair of dancers, but if there had been twice as many old Fezziwig and Mrs. Fezziwig would have been a match for them.

When the clock struck eleven, the ball broke up. Mr. and Mrs. Fezziwig took their stations on either side of the door and wished every person a Merry Christmas.

The Ghost said, "To make these silly folks so happy he has spent but a few pounds of your mortal money."

Scrooge said, "The happiness he gives is quite as great as if it cost a fortune." He felt the Spirit's glance and stopped.

"My time grows short," observed the Spirit. "Quick!"

This was not addressed to Scrooge, or to any one whom he could see, but it produced an immediate effect.

For again he saw himself. He was older now; a man in the prime of life. He was not alone, but with a fair young girl, in whose eyes there were tears. She said softly to Scrooge's former self, "Another idol has displaced me."

"What idol has displaced you?"

"A golden one. I have seen your nobler aspirations fall off one by one, until the master-passion, Gain, engrosses you."

For again he saw himself. He was older now; a man in the prime of life. He was not alone, but with a fair young girl, in whose eyes there were tears. She said softly to Scrooge's former self, "Another idol has displaced me."

"What idol has displaced you?"

"A golden one. I have seen your nobler aspirations fall off one by one, until the master-passion, Gain, engrosses you."

Scrooge said, "I have grown wiser but I have not sought release from our engagement."

She answered, "If you were free today, I do not believe you would choose a dowerless girl. I release you from our engagement."

Scrooge awoke in his own bedroom. He saw bright light shining from the next room. There he saw the Ghost of Christmas Present.

"Touch my robe!" the Spirit commanded.

Scrooge did as he was told, and held it fast. The room and its contents all vanished instantly, and they passed on, invisible, straight to the house of Scrooge's clerk upon a snowy Christmas morning.

Bob entered, his threadbare clothes brushed to look seasonable, and Tiny Tim upon his shoulders, carrying his crutch.

"Touch my robe!" the Spirit commanded.

Scrooge did as he was told, and held it fast. The room and its contents all vanished instantly, and they passed on, invisible, straight to the house of Scrooge's clerk upon a snowy Christmas morning.

Bob entered, his threadbare clothes brushed to look seasonable, and Tiny Tim upon his shoulders, carrying his crutch.

Mrs. Cratchit and the little Cratchits all had their chores in preparing the Christmas feast that centered on a goose. Its tenderness and flavor, size and cheapness, were the themes of universal admiration.

Eked out by apple-sauce and mashed potatoes, it was a sufficient dinner for the whole family. The youngest Cratchits in particular were steeped in sage and onion to the eyebrows!

The feast was climaxed by a wonderful pudding and a round of toasts. "God bless us every one!" said Tiny Tim.

Bob toasted, "I'll give you Mr. Scrooge, the Founder of the Feast!"

There was nothing of high mark in this celebration, but they were happy, grateful, pleased with one another, and contented with the time.

It was a great surprise to Scrooge, as this scene vanished, to hear a hearty laugh and a greater surprise to recognize it as his own nephew's. Scrooge's niece by marriage laughed just as heartily.

"He said that Christmas was a humbug, as I live!" cried Scrooge's nephew. "He believed it too!"

"More shame for him, Fred!" said Scrooge's niece. She was very pretty, exceedingly pretty.

"He's a comical old fellow," said Scrooge's nephew. "His offenses carry their own punishment. He suffers by his ill whims. He chooses to dislike us and won't come and dine with us. I have nothing to say against him."

After tea they had music and later they played at games.

Scrooge and the Spirit left the party. Much they saw, and far they went, and many homes they visited, but always with a happy end.

The bell struck twelve and the Ghost of Christmas Present was replaced by a solemn phantom. It was draped and hooded, coming like a mist along the ground towards Scrooge. Slowly, gravely, and silently it approached: the Ghost of Christmas Yet to Come. When it came near him, Scrooge bent down upon his knee; for in the air through which this Spirit moved it seemed to scatter gloom and mystery.

They went to a low shop in an obscure part of town where iron, old rags, bottles, bones, and other junk were bought. A grey-haired man sat at a table. Two women and a man in black entered carrying bundles of stolen goods for sale.

Scrooge thought the goods looked familiar. They spoke very disrespectfully of the former owner, apparently departed in death.

The scene changed and Scrooge saw the body of this plundered unknown man lying on a bare bed, unwatched, unwept, and uncared for. Scrooge tried but couldn't bring himself to remove the sheet from the man's face.

Scrooge begged the Spirit to please reveal to him just one person who showed some tenderness connected with a death.

The Ghost took him to the Cratchit house. The family was still and sad. Tiny Tim was nowhere to be seen. Bob was the saddest; he had just returned from a visit to the graveyard.

Scrooge begged the Ghost to tell him what man that was, with the covered face lying dead and uncared for. The Ghost took him to a dismal, wretched churchyard. The Spirit stood amongst the graves and pointed down to One.

Scrooge pleaded with the Ghost, "Spirit! hear me! I am not the man I was. Assure me that I yet may change these shadows you have shown me. I will not shut out the lessons the Christmas Spirits teach. Tell me I may sponge away the writing on this stone!"

Scrooge found himself back in his own bed. He prayed to have his fate reversed. He ran to the window. A boy on the street assured him it was Christmas day. The Three Spirits had come and gone in one night. He had a chance to make amends.

Scrooge had the boy deliver a prize turkey to the Cratchits. It was twice the size of Tiny Tim. Bob Cratchit would not know who sent it.

Scrooge dressed himself all in his best and went out into the streets. He regarded every one with a delighted smile. He received many greetings of "Merry Christmas!"

In the afternoon he turned his steps towards his nephew's house.

He passed the door a dozen times before he had the courage to go up and knock. But he made a dash and did it.

"It's I, your uncle Scrooge. I have come to dinner. Will you let me in, Fred?"

Let him in! It is a mercy Fred didn't shake his arm off. Wonderful party, wonderful games, wonderful happiness. But Scrooge was early at the office next morning to be there first and catch Bob Cratchit coming late! Bob was full eighteen minutes and a half behind his time. He was on his stool in a jiffy.

"Hallo!" growled Scrooge. "What do you mean by coming here at this time of day?"

"I am very sorry, sir. I *am* behind my time."

"You are? Yes. I think you are. Step this way if you please."

"It shall not be repeated. I was making rather merry yesterday, sir."

"I am not going to stand this sort of thing any longer. And therefore," Scrooge continued, leaping from his stool, "and therefore I am about to raise your salary!"

Bob trembled.

"A Merry Christmas, Bob!" said Scrooge, with an earnestness that could not be mistaken. "A Merrier Christmas, Bob, my good fellow, than I have given you for many a year! I'll raise your salary, and endeavor to assist your struggling family, and we will discuss your affairs this very afternoon. Make up the fires, and buy a second coal-scuttle before you dot another *i*, Bob Cratchit!"

From that day forth, Scrooge helped the Cratchit family and became like a second father to Tiny Tim. It was ever afterwards said of Scrooge that he knew how to keep Christmas well. And so, as Tiny Tim observed, God Bless Us, Every One!